Milly and Molly

For my grandchildren
Thomas, Harry, Ella and Madeleine

Milly and Molly Go Camping

Copyright © Milly Molly Books, 2003

Gill Pittar and Cris Morrell assert the moral right to
be recognized as the author and illustrator of this work.

Published by
Milly Molly Books
P O Box 539
Gisborne, New Zealand
email: books@millymolly.com

Printed by Rhythm Consolidated Berhad, Malaysia

ISBN: 1-86972-003-2

10   9   8   7   6   5   4   3   2   1

Milly and Molly
Go Camping

"We may look different
but we feel the same."

Every summer Milly and Molly pulled the
old tent out of the coat closet under the
stairs.

Their dads always helped them put it up.
Then Milly and Molly filled it with all their
favorite things.

The pillows off their beds.
A big, colorful patchwork blanket.
An old wooden box turned upside down,
for secret things. A tin of chocolate brownies
and their reading books and dolls.
And a flashlight, just in case they had the
courage to camp out for a night.

The first time they camped on the lawn
in the front garden.

The second time they camped in the back
garden under the lemon tree.

And the third time they camped outside
the garden fence and stayed out for half a
night.

This time Milly and Molly decided they would
camp out for a whole night.

Milly's dad said, "I'll believe it when I see it."
Molly's dad said, "I'll eat my hat if you two
camp out all night."
And Jack and Tom said, "The bears will eat
you for dinner." That made Milly and Molly
all the more determined.

After their dads left, Milly and Molly
worked busily to get their camp in order.

They set up the box and put the flashlight
where they could easily reach it.

When everything was done, they ate their
picnic dinner. They picked up every crumb,
so as not to tempt the bears.

Soon the light began to fade and the
shadows grew longer. Milly began to shiver.
"Whose idea was this?"
"Yours," said Molly.

Before it was completely dark, Milly and Molly
laced themselves tightly in to their tent.
They snuggled down to read, using their
flashlight to give them light.

Then they heard a shuffle. Then silence.

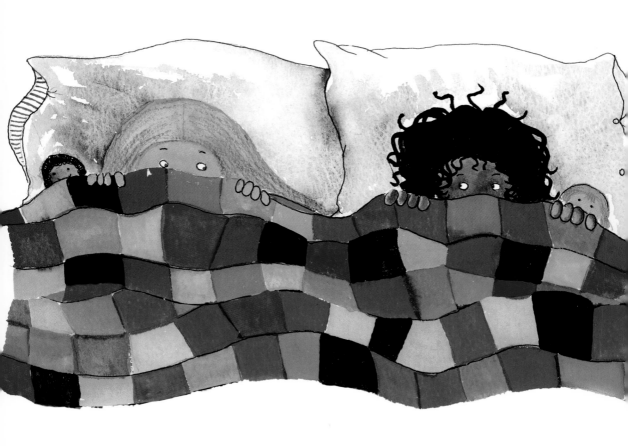

"It was your idea."
"It was yours," whispered Molly.

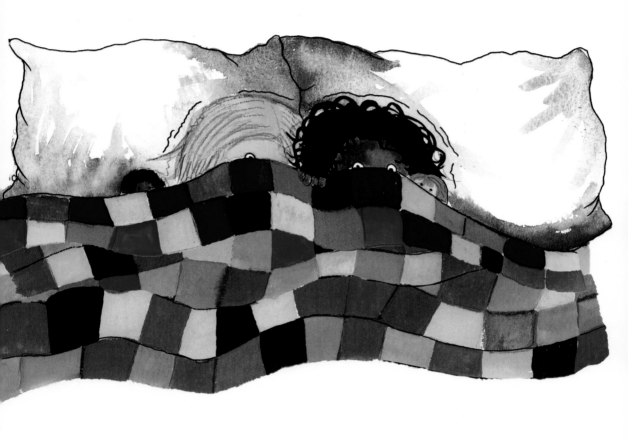

Then there was a scratching at the canvas.
Milly couldn't find her voice.
Nor could Molly.

They clung together and waited, hardly
able to breathe. There was a long silence.
Then they saw an eye peering through the
crack between the laces. It shone red in
the flashlight.

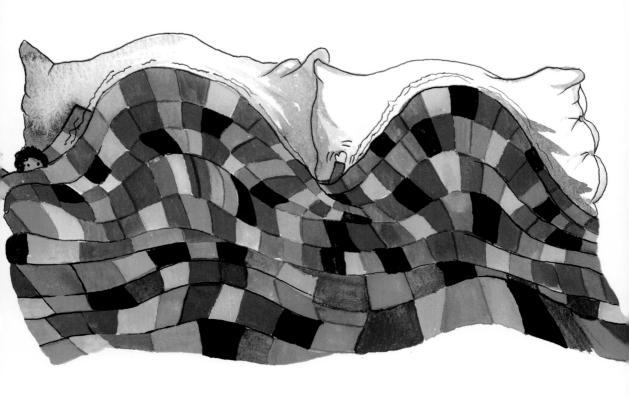

Milly and Molly dived under their
patchwork blanket and prepared to die.

The animal pounced. Milly and Molly
started to scream ... and thrash ... and
scream.

Suddenly all was quiet. They opened their eyes but there was nothing to see except an empty silence... and a small hump in the patchwork blanket. Very slowly the hump began to move, and who should appear?

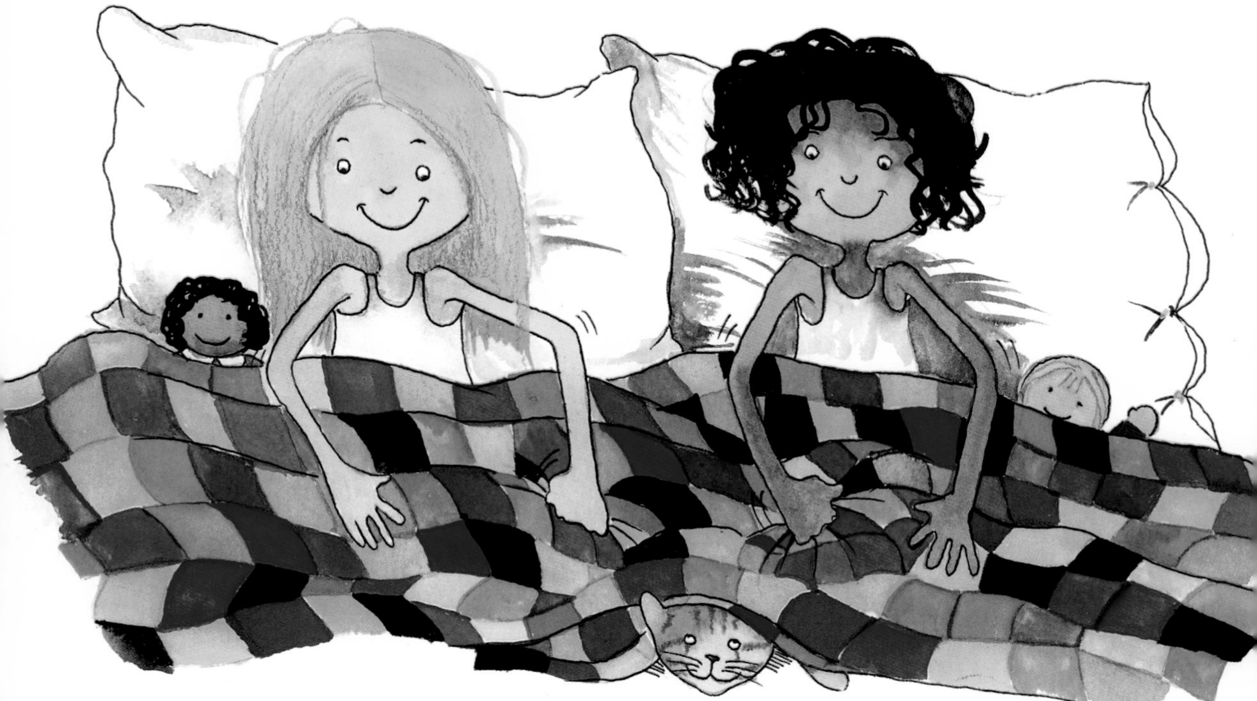

But Tom Cat!

Milly and Molly clung to Tom Cat with relief
and collapsed with exhaustion.

When they woke with the birds in the morning, Milly and Molly couldn't believe they had camped out all night.

"Tom and Harry won't believe us," said Milly.

"They will when they see Dad eat his hat," said Molly.

Milly and Molly Go Camping

The value implicitly expressed in this story is 'courage and determination' the ability to face fear; to be firmly decided.

Milly and Molly camped out for the night with determination and courage. Their dads and Tom and Jack tested their determination while Tom Cat tested their courage.

"We may look different but we feel the same".

B O O K S

Other picture books in the Milly, Molly series include:

- Milly, Molly and Jimmy's Seeds   ISBN 1-86972-000-8
- Milly, Molly and Beefy   ISBN 1-86972-006-7
- Milly, Molly and Taffy Bogle   ISBN 1-86972-001-6
- Milly, Molly and Oink   ISBN 1-86972-002-4
- Milly and Molly Betelgeuse   ISBN 1-86972-005-9
- Milly, Molly and Pet Day   ISBN 1-86972-004-0